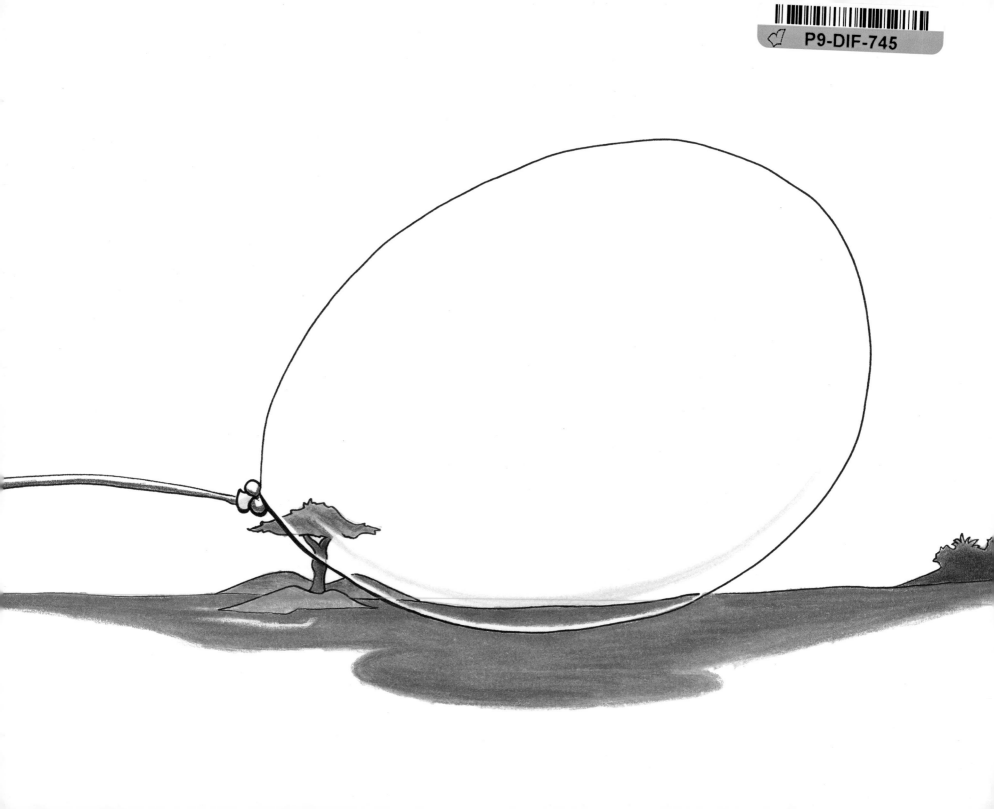

THE LEGEND OF Papa Balloon

C. R. McClure
Illustrations by
Steven Kernen

Schiffer
Publishing Ltd®
4880 Lower Valley Road • Atglen, PA 19310

Published by Schiffer Publishing, Ltd.
4880 Lower Valley Road
Atglen, PA 19310
Phone: (610) 593-1777; Fax: (610) 593-2002
E-mail: Info@schifferbooks.com

For the largest selection of fine reference books on this and related subjects, please visit our website at www.schifferbooks.com.
You may also write for a free catalog.

This book may be purchased from the publisher.
Please try your bookstore first.

We are always looking for people to write books on new and related subjects. If you have an idea for a book, please contact us at proposals@schifferbooks.com

Schiffer Books are available at special discounts for bulk purchases for sales promotions or premiums. Special editions, including personalized covers, corporate imprints, and excerpts can be created in large quantities for special needs. For more information contact the publisher.

In Europe, Schiffer books are distributed by
Bushwood Books
6 Marksbury Ave.
Kew Gardens
Surrey TW9 4JF England
Phone: 44 (0) 20 8392 8585; Fax: 44 (0) 20 8392 9876
E-mail: info@bushwoodbooks.co.uk
Website: www.bushwoodbooks.co.uk

To my loving and supportive family,
without whom none of this would be possible

– C.R. McClure

To my family, who keep my pencils and me
sharp and my colors and me bright.

– Steven Kernen

There was once a beautiful land which was full of life,
light, and lots and lots of colored balloons.

Everyone loved the Light because it gave them life
and they used balloons to express how they felt.

There were four villages in this land and each believed that their way
of loving the Light was the best and that any other way wasn't right.

Into this land appeared a man.

He was discovered sleeping under a tree by some children
from each village who had been playing together.

They woke the man up and asked him his name.

He said that everyone called him "Papa."

"Papa what?" they said, and at that he took off the hat he
was wearing, and out from under it floated a crystal clear balloon.

"Papa Balloon!" they exclaimed,
and so he was called from then on.

Now, the balloon which he produced was unusual
because all the other balloons in the land were a certain color:
red, green, blue, or purple.

Yet his you could see right through.

The children were eager to take their new friend
to meet their parents and so off they went.

First, they came to the village of Red.

All of the people were busy building
things out of red balloons
to help other people.

They were building houses,
hospitals, schools, and many
other helpful things.

This made Papa smile.

When the leaders of the village came out to meet Papa, they told him that the "Big Book of Red" told them that being good and helping other people was the best way to make the Light happy and that all other ways weren't as good.

"What do you think?"

"It depends on why you act," said Papa.

This made sense to some of the people and so they followed him to the next village— the village of Green.

Now, in the village of Green, everyone was busy making balloon objects…
especially Suns, Moons, and little dogs.

The Suns and Moons, because they represented the Light and little dogs because once, a long time ago, a very special little dog had loved being in the Light so much that whenever the Sun would rise or the Moon come out, he would do a little dance. And the people found that loving the dog made them happy and feel closer to the Light, too.

When the leaders of the village of Green asked
Papa what he thought he said…
"It depends on how you feel."

Many people liked his answer and
followed him to the next village—
the village of Blue.

The village of Blue was very unique, because most of the people lived in big blue hot air balloons from which they could see far and wide.

They lived in the balloons because, long ago, a very smart person had taught the village that studying the Light helped you get closer to it and better understand what it is and who you are.

The leaders, from up in their balloons, asked loudly what Papa thought. And Papa bellowed back, "It depends on how you think!" Many people liked what he said, got down from their balloons and followed him to the last village—the village of Purple.

Now the village of Purple was very different from the other villages because there were very few houses. Mostly the villagers sat around very still and quiet. Some in the sun, some under trees, and they concentrated on blowing up a purple balloon and then letting it deflate…blowing up the balloon and then letting it deflate. Because, for them, this was all they really needed to feel at peace and be at one with the Light.

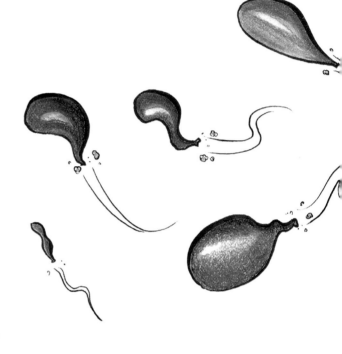

This time, the crowd of followers which was around Papa asked him what he thought and he replied, "It depends on who you are."

But the crowd wanted more, and they kept asking him in which village were the people living the best lives.

Papa turned to them and said that "it depends on how you act, feel, think, or just are."

But the people wanted a clearer answer, and so Papa took off his hat and once again the crystal clear balloon floated out. It floated high into the air and soon caught the Light.

And through it, everyone saw all the colors: red, green, blue, and purple, plus ones they hadn't seen before.

And those gathered around realized that the Light contained all the colors and that it falls on everyone equally...no matter who they are or where they live.

As the people realized this,
the balloon suddenly popped.

And when they looked down…
Papa Balloon was gone.

But the people of the Land of Light were not sad, for they realized that he was of the Light, just like everyone, from every village.

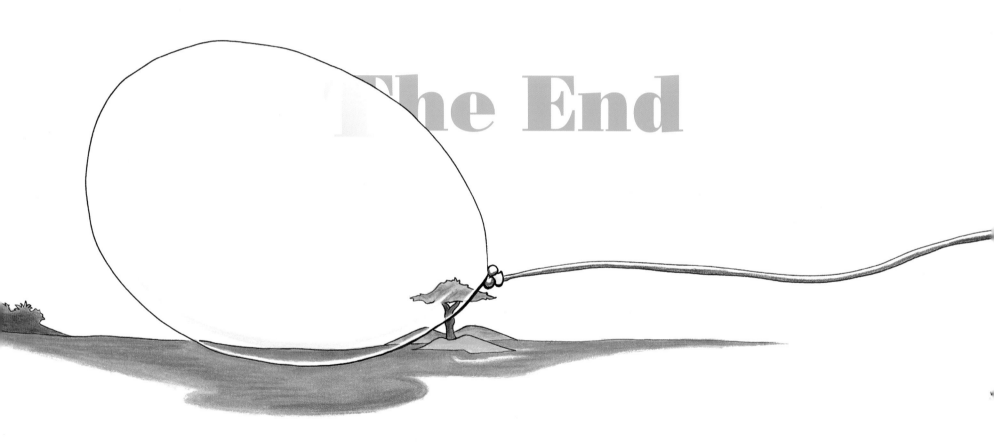

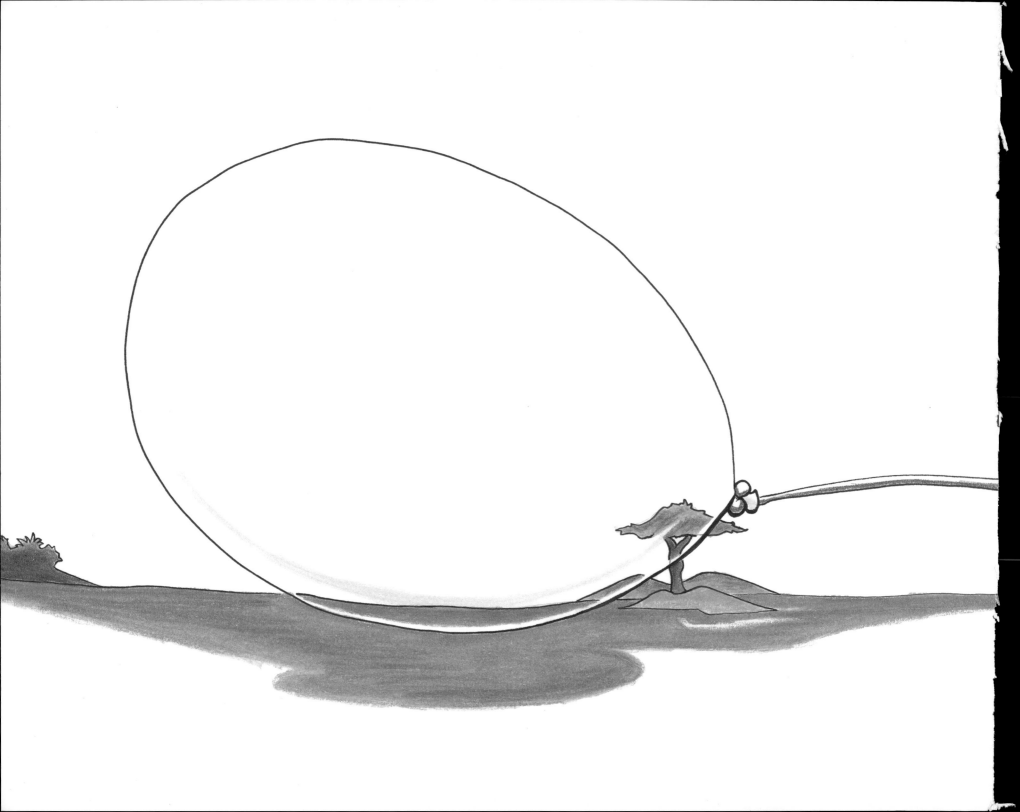